A Cornish Odyssey

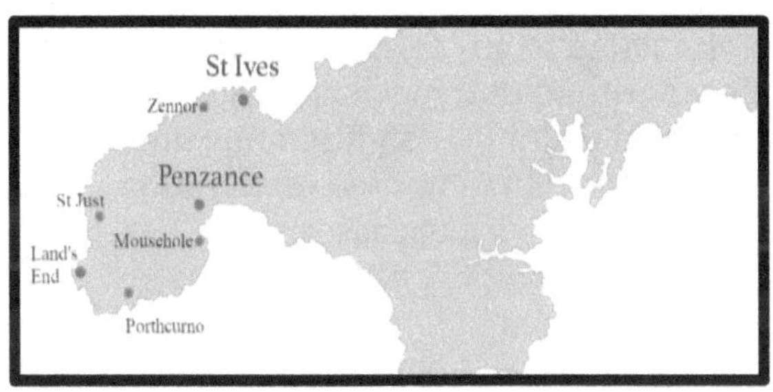

BY

AXEL FORRESTER

ISBN: 9781739653934

Chapter One

I didn't know the first thing about Cornwall before I went there, and that was probably for the best. When my finger landed on Penzance, in Land's End, Cornwall, the westernmost part of England, I knew that's where my adventure would start. Penzance! It even sounded like adventure. Pirates of Penzance! This was exactly what I needed for my summer holiday this year. As a high school art teacher in North Hollywood, I was in desperate need of change. It was getting harder each year to convince myself that I had the life I wanted.

My parents were both teachers. I had three older sisters. Teacher. Teacher. Teacher. Check. Check. Check. As the youngest and the only son, I was determined to break with this relentless pattern. Cultivating an Oscar Wilde look, I wore a black beret to high school, and for good measure, a cape. My parents declared this to be a phase, saying it too would pass. They liked to remind me that up until this point I had been sure I was going to be a professional snowboarder.

I reminded them in turn, that it was their fault it hadn't happened. They were the ones who made me live miles away from the nearest ski slopes.

While I wasn't Valedictorian of my high school, like my sister, I did get the class award for 'most likely to do something creative.' During my last year as an art major at Cal State Northridge, my older sister, Greta, suggested I go an extra year and get a teaching credential, just in case. 'In case of what?' I had asked. 'Oh, you know, in case you want to eat.'

The arguments at the dinner table got more heated. One night, my father, a political science professor at UCLA, quoted John Adams at me. 'I must study politics and war, that my son may have the liberty to study mathematics, philosophy, and art.' I responded with a quote of my own, from Benjamin Franklin. 'Many people die at twenty-five and aren't buried until they are seventy-five.'

While I won that battle, I lost the war. I knew I wasn't cut out to starve, or borrow money from my father, so I caved and got the credential. It landed me a job at an arts and science high school in North Hollywood (Noho). I taught photography. It was brutal my first year, but gradually, I nailed it. The one perk of this job was that I had summers off, and long breaks to make my own art, the photographs I developed in the darkroom I set up in my apartment.

The arts faculty at NoHo Arts and Science might have looked artsy, but I was the real deal. My photographs were edgy. Dark. Very dark. I had a one-man show at ArtHYPE. Some of my students came to the opening. Some girls anyway. The boys could not have cared less.

This year I turned forty. Yeah. I know. Unbelievable, right? I'd been teaching there for fifteen years and, I'll be honest with you, it was not going well. There were grey hairs at my temples, flab around my waist, and I had jowls. Clearly, the toxic school environment was to blame. There were bells every hour to jolt us on to the next activity. Everything was so scheduled, so over organised. The place was totally risk-averse. The faculty meetings went on to infinity.

And there were these soul... crushing... pep rallies. Watching the football team warm-up was, in my opinion, a torturous waste of time and, frankly, humiliating. Parading all that equipment in front of us was meant to drive home the fact that the sports budget was ten times greater than the art or science budget.

Cornwall, on the other hand, sounded like just the sort of place to get my mojo back. A walking trip along the Cornish coast would revive me! The stunning scenery. The fresh air. Cornish pasties! It would give me a whole new perspective, ignite my creativity, and restore my balance. Best of all, I could visit an exotic country without having to learn a foreign language! I'd read up on the place and learn things. Cornwall must have had pirates. Pirates of Penzance! I'd photograph the landscape and the colourful Cornish people. The new digital camera I just bought would be my faithful companion. Maybe I'd write a grant when I got back, to fund an exhibit of the photos. It would look good on the old resume. My department chair, Bill Bentley, would like that. He was always telling me to take more initiative. So, I'd take initiative! I'd go to Cornwall!

An intensive Google search brought me to the website of a company called The Intrepid Traveller. Their website was reassuringly old fashioned. Quaint. I fired off an email, telling them I wanted to walk the coast of Cornwall, from Penzance to St Ives, in five days, in early July.

A chap named Graeme got back to me via email and said he could arrange for me to stay at highly rated, private B&B's at Mousehole, Porthcurno, St Just, Zennor and St Ives. Breakfast included. Full English. Full English? Did this mean my hosts would be 100% English? Well, why not? Give me the Full English! He also said my bags would be transported from place to place. How convenient!

Graeme called the following week. He sounded full English.

'So, you're an American? What state are you in?'

'California.'

'And may I ask your age?'

'Thirty-five.' There was nothing wrong with a little white lie. Everyone lies about their age in California. It's expected.

'Your weight and height?'

'Whoa! Dude! You NEVER ask someone's weight in California!'

There was a momentary silence as he gathered himself.

'Well, uh...we need to get an idea of your fitness level, for our insurance, Sir.'

'Oh, I'm fit. No worries there.'

Graeme took a deep breath.

'This walk is listed on our website as moderate, but as an American, you'll find it difficult.'

I laughed.

He went on.

'In our experience, Americans are not used to the strenuous nature of our coastal walks. There are a lot of ups and downs, and rough walking. You'll probably need to do some training before you come. Do you take the stairs at work?'

'I told you. I'm fit. Very fit, in fact.'

'Yes, well, the first day is fourteen miles. But don't worry. You can always take the bus.'

'I am in tip-top condition, Graeme. I take frequent walks in the High Sierras. I've noticed that Cornwall hasn't any mountains to speak of.

I will have no trouble with this coast walk, I assure you.' I thought I was sounding a little English now myself.

Graeme went quiet again. Then, he cleared his throat.

'Right. I'll be sending the safety information to you in a few days. Please read all of it carefully, sign the waivers, and be sure to get everything on the equipment list. You'll have to be prepared for all weather.'

'In July?'

'Especially in July.'

'OK. Fine.'

'And remember. You can always–'

'Take the bus. Yes, I remember, but I wouldn't dream of it!'

'As you wish. Good-Bye, Mr Decker.'

'Grant. Call me Grant.'

'Good-Bye, Mr Decker.'

I hung up the phone. There was no way in hell I was going to take a bus on my walking adventure around Cornwall. I'd show this Graeme person what I was made of. Not all Americans were obese and lazy. Some of us were fit, intrepid travellers.

It was May. I didn't get to the High Sierras that weekend, or the next, but I did see a movie called High Sierra, which was great. Humphrey Bogart stars in this classic noir film about a bank robber on the lam in the High Sierras with his mother, his associates, and the loot. He meets a beautiful, young, crippled woman and must make a terrible choice. I won't spoil the ending for you.

At the end of June, the school was, once again, the scene of mass panic attacks as students ran around seeking help with their over-ambitious final projects. At the end, there were awards ceremonies, more awards ceremonies, and farewell parties. At the very end, there was the grading. All our art students got 'A's'. It was more or less expected. The art teachers just had to find a way to justify these grades with numbers. On the last day, in the last hour, I was there in my office, as usual, adding everything up and dividing by prime numbers until things came out right. When my grades were finally uploaded, I shut down the computer, secured my classroom door and headed home, free at last!

I changed into my running clothes and drove up to Rocky Peak Park. It was a lot closer than the High Sierras and would do for one last shot at training. Parking by the side of the road, I locked the door and went for a five-mile hike, my keys jiggling in my pocket. It seemed like hours, because–it was hours. When I finally limped back to the car, I had a stitch in my side and was breathing hard. My training done, I gave myself an 'A,' for effort and drove home, sweaty and satisfied. It was June 30th. The next day I was on a plane bound for London.

Chapter Two

I had to pay extra to have my cell phone work in the UK, but Graeme insisted this was necessary. He was going to call me every night to be sure I'd made it safely to each place. You would think I was on an expedition to climb Mount Everest. At first, I thought this was quite English of him, and very sweet. But then, cynically, I reminded myself that he wouldn't get good reviews on Trip Advisor if I went over the cliff.

On the plane, I skimmed the safety instructions. The packet was two inches thick and covered everything from bee stings to snake bites (Cornwall has adders!) and how to deal with hurricane-force winds. I hoped the airport at Heathrow would have a shop where I could buy a compass, a whistle, a rain poncho, a sun hat, a first aid kit, sun cream, a signal flare, a small shovel, a Swiss army knife, 24KN 8-10mm climbing rope and all the other things on this very long list. I also hoped Graeme was just being Full English about this walk, exaggerating the dangers to show how prepared he was. I didn't find much on the list at the airport, but I did find a wonderful book on pirates.

Fun fact number one. Did you know the most successful pirate in history was a woman? Madame Ching Shih. She terrorized the China Seas. She also arranged clemency for her vast crew of pirates, hundreds of them, as a sort of retirement program. The drawing of her in the book reminded me of my high school geometry teacher, Mrs Lee. She terrorized the whole eighth grade.

After one night at a cheap hotel near Heathrow, I got the early morning train to Penzance. Seven hours. I didn't think England was big enough for a train journey that lasted that long. I got a lot of reading done. Cornwall had their fair share of pirates.

Fun fact number two. Did you know pirates voted for their captains? They were determined to do things differently from the English Navy, which was, let's face it, harsh. These men were taking initiative, going on their adventures. Inspiring! Democratic! When I emerged from the train in the town of Penzance, the sun was shining and all my troubles seemed like they were on the other side of the world, because– they were.

Penzance certainly rallied around the pirate theme. Sitting on my bench with some fish and chips, I spotted touristy pirate paraphernalia all over the place, mostly for children and old people. But being an intrepid traveller, I was not fooled by the plastic swords and fake pirate gold. I bought only one, practical souvenir: a black eye patch. I thought it might protect one of my eyes from the seagulls of exceptional size, having a go at my fish and chips. They were as big as chickens!

To avoid injury, I ducked into the back of a cab, a beat-up old hatchback with a yellowing plastic sign attached to the roof, which read, Pirate Taxi. I asked the driver to take me to Mousehole. The gnarly old man guffawed while slapping the fur-lined steering wheel. Turning to me with a crooked smile and two missing teeth, he said:

'MAOZALL. It's MAOZALL, mate.'

'No, I want Mousehole. That's what it says on the map.'

He shook his head, laughed at me again and soon unintelligible words came flying out of his mouth as we sped off. It sounded like no language I had ever heard before. He kept staring at me in the rear-view mirror, shaking his head and mumbling. I gave him the Full American.

When I saw the sign that said Mousehole, I felt reassured. I wasn't being abducted after all. We were in the right place. I showed him the address and he took me through the village. It had streets so narrow, that I was sure we were going to crash into one of those white-washed stone buildings. We took another turn, climbed the hill above the town and soon were in what looked like a nice little neighbourhood with houses slightly bigger and considerably further apart.

After waving the taxi off, I rang the doorbell and was greeted by a trim little housewife, wearing a clean white apron over a matching green skirt and sweater ensemble. She also wore stockings and light blue terrycloth slippers. I was sure this couldn't be the right B&B. If it was, then Graeme and I had very different notions of 'high grade' accommodation. This was, embarrassingly, like an average, or even below-average family home. Was this woman so hard up that she needed to rent a room to strangers?

I was shown to a bedroom where there was a single bed with a thin comforter that had race cars on it, a wood desk with a chair, a cheap wood dresser, and a homemade bookshelf that was crammed with comic books and video games. Nintendo. Atari. Super Mario. A child's room. I wondered what she'd done with the child. Had he grown up and moved out? It seemed unlikely if the video games were still here. I was trying to imagine what happened to him, putting my things away, when suddenly, my hostess stuck her head in the room. It felt like I was fifteen again, annoyed at the intrusion of my mother.

'What time would you like breakfast?'

'Oh, whatever's good for you.' I tried not to imagine this woman in her 1950s morning gown.

'Eight o'clock all right?'

'Sure.'

'How'd you like your eggs?'

I was going to tell her to surprise me, but I suspected, her being Full English, this might make her nervous.

'Could you do them over easy?'

'You mean runny?'

'Yes.' I smiled. Blend in. 'Runny.'

'Of course.'

She sounded professional, as if she had run a B&B all her life and her family was the sideline. But what had she done with them? I saw no one else around. No husband, no children. Maybe they were all staying with relatives somewhere else.

'Uh, is it too late to find something to eat in town?'

'There's a chip shop by the harbour. With local fish. It should be open.'

'Great. Thanks.'

I got out my wallet with the fresh pound notes and was off. After walking down the hill, it wasn't long before I was back in the tiny streets of the fishing village with the little shops by the harbour and the smallest cottages I'd ever seen. The seagulls here were so enormous that they made the houses look even smaller. Standing in the middle of one of the cobble-stoned streets I extended both arms and could touch the houses on either side. Moments later a mini-bus—no, make that a micro mini-bus, came careening around the corner. I just managed to jump over a low white picket fence, narrowly avoiding death in Mousehole. Death in Mousehole. It sounded like the title of an Agatha Christie novel.

Once I recovered from the shock, I found the chip shop and asked the man serving me my dinner on a sheet of newsprint how he said this town's name.

'MAOZALL.'

The whole town was in on it. Their little joke. I wandered around this excellent re-creation of a seventeenth-century fishing village and bought a children's book about Mousehole with beautiful illustrations. The story was charming. At the end of the book was a description of a Christmas tradition which still supposedly takes place at dusk, on Christmas Eve. People stand on the edge of the semi-circular harbour, holding candles to light the way for the fishermen coming back from the sea. At midnight, the whole village shares a traditional fish stew to celebrate the safe return of the fishermen. I was imagining the whole village, their faces lit by candles, sharing in the warmth of the meal together, when my cell phone rang.

'Hello?'

'Hi there. It's Graeme. Are you in MAOZALL?'

'Why didn't you tell me how to say the name of this town?'

'What?'

'Never mind. Yes. I'm here in MAOZALL.'

'Everything all right?'

'Delightful!'

'Ready for a long day tomorrow?'

'I am.'

'Right, then. Speak to you tomorrow night.'

And the line went dead. Graeme certainly wasn't going to waste any time with chit chat. He merely wanted to be sure I was alive.

*

The next morning, I was dressed and ready at eight sharp. I wandered into the living room where a dining room table had been set up and five people were sitting there, chatting to one another, apparently waiting on me. The table looked like the scene of a Thanksgiving dinner. There were baked beans, fried mushrooms, stewed tomatoes, a plate of black hamburger patties, sausages, several neat little silver thingies with wheat toast standing up in them, and butter and jam in little flowered dishes.

Everyone at the table already had eggs on their plate and was passing around everything else.

As I sat down, my hostess, in another timeless fifties outfit, with an apron, served up two 'runny' eggs on my plate. I thanked her and looked around the table. Everyone here was an adult and looked vaguely uncomfortable. Each person nodded in greeting, signalling that they were guests like me, only too polite to intrude on my privacy by introducing themselves. Full English!

'Would you like yoghurt and cereal?' asked our hostess, as if I would still be hungry after all this food. 'We have a selection over here.' She swung her arm out to the table behind her, where, as promised, there were six kinds of cereal and four kinds of yoghurt, a dish of prunes and one of canned mixed fruits. I wondered how anyone could eat so much for breakfast. We also had our choice of several kinds of tea, coffee, orange, or pineapple juice. When I didn't partake of the burned meat patties, the man sitting next to me said, 'Not a fan of blood sausage?' Good God. I shook my head and smiled. He tutted. 'Can't say you've had the Full English without these!' I blinked and silently reached for the toast. Blood sausages. The Full English. Why haven't these rather important terms been explained, Graeme?

After thanking my hostess, I waddled out of MAOZALL, dangerously overstuffed. Try as I might, I could not figure out how she made any money. We each easily ate £50 worth of food, the whole cost of the night's accommodation. At the top of the hill, I was stopped by the incredible sight of Mousehole, the loveliest fishing village I had ever laid eyes on. Rays of the sun were piercing the clouds in long celestial streams, creating islands of light on the azure sea. I listened as the wind whistled past me. It was so...real. So authentic. We had nothing like this in California. I liked Mousehole. It was still a fishing village, for the most part. A quiet place.

I reflected and took out my map to figure out where I was going next. Porthcurno. I had a very long way to go, but it was another marvellous sunny day, and I had the enthusiasm of an intrepid traveller. I was on my way!

The trail ambled along for several hours and then suddenly got very narrow and steep. I felt like a goat going up and then down the rocky path, slipping and sliding. I had a few close calls.

At one point I was hundreds of feet up and below me I could see crashing waves and a pebbly beach. It was very easy to imagine old three-masted ships smashing to smithereens on those black rocks, the locals gleefully picking up everything that washed up on the shore.

Fun fact number three: Smuggling was the number one occupation of the Cornish people back then. Though harsh penalties made it difficult, this was sometimes the only way to feed their families.

There was plenty of time to think as I walked on this path. Putting one foot in front of the other, this dull repetition reminded me of my job. Every day was the same, every week, every month, every year. School may have been hell for my students, but it was a double hell for me. I had never liked school. What was I doing repeating it? Over and over? There was a ring of failure in this for me. I never even went to my high school graduation and now I'd been to fifteen of them. The irony of it. They were compulsory for teachers. I had twenty-seven more to go until I retired.

I was exhausted by the time I got to Lamorna Cove. The water was the colour of emeralds. There was a bench, where I sat down, took a long drink of water, and reached into my rucksack for the newsprint wrapped fish sandwich I'd bought in MAOZALL. It was delicious, but I couldn't fully enjoy it. A seagull was watching me with angry little red eyes.

After my lunch, I unfolded the map on the bench and calculated how far I'd come. It was two miles. Nooooooo. That couldn't be right. I checked the scale on the map again. Damn. Just like my job. So much more misery ahead. It was going to be a long day. It was noon and I had twelve more miles to go. I wiped the salt from my lips, took another swig of water and marched back to the path. There was nothing to do but get on with it and look for some adventure. It had to be here somewhere.

There were lots of bushes, I can tell you. Almost no trees. Little yellow flowers hung on these bushes, and I've since learned to call them gorse bushes. They are everywhere. The path was always before me, up and down these steep hills and valleys. It was hot. I drank all my water by mile ten and my feet had developed sizable blisters. I came to an area of the path that became densely wooded, but not with the kind of trees I expected in England. It began looking tropical, with palm trees and other lush vegetation. It was as if I was in some other part of the world altogether, until I spotted a red phone box, right there in the middle of this jungle. I took a picture. This, I would tell my students, was contrast. A red English telephone box in a green jungle. My first iconic photo of the trip. My heart lifted. I was on to something.

Further on the trail, there was a small sign, hand painted, that read: 'Cream Tea.' There was a little arrow pointing to the right. I followed the sign, with a sense of foreboding, half expecting to find the mad hatter from Alice in Wonderland.

I soon came to a white cottage with a thatched roof, sitting on a hill with a view of the sea. And what a view! The blue-green ocean was framed by palms, bean trees, yucca plants and red lilies. I took a few snaps, but when I gazed at the pictures, even I didn't believe they were taken in England.

Another sign directed me to the garden where I found an open window to a kitchen. There was a friendly-looking fellow in a striped apron, taking tea orders from a man speaking

German. I stood behind him in front of the window and noticed a small placard saying: 'Best chocolate cake in England.' Well.

I will confess right here and now that while I love the idea of tea, especially when it includes cake, I don't like tea itself. To me, it's just hot water with a brown crayon dipped in it. Too weak to mean anything to my tastebuds. And this claim that you should drink something hot when you are feeling hot just seems idiotic to me. It is not what my body cries out for. Therefore, I glanced at the menu and was pleased to see freshly squeezed orange juice on offer. That's what I ordered with my chocolate cake. My blood sugar would be off the charts, but what the hell. It was my holiday.

After ordering, I sat down on one of the padded garden chairs, removed my khaki waterproof hat and revelled in the gentle sea breeze caressing my tired body. This was exquisite relief. Heavenly. The only thing that disrupted my peace was the sound of Germans chatting away next to me. They were sitting as a group—tanned, robust, and obnoxiously healthy looking. They had grey hair. Sagging necks. They must have been in their sixties, but they were in fabulous shape from the neck down. I closed my eyes and tried to ignore them.

The cake was every bit as good as advertised. Moist. Chocolatey. Not too sweet, just right. Perfect texture. I wish now I had taken a picture of it. The orange juice was perfect too. Where did they get oranges in England? Were they from Spain? Delicious. It stood out as the most perfect moment of my trip so far. I didn't want to leave this spot, but knew I had to move on if I was going to get to Porthcurno by dark. On my way out, I stopped by the window and thanked the man and told him how much I enjoyed the cake. He was friendly and I lingered to ask if he lived here year-round. He laughed politely, as if I were a stranger.

'No, my wife and I live in Spain ten months of the year. We're only here July and August when the tourists come.'

'Ah. Is that where you get the oranges then?'

'No, we got these at Morrison's, in Penzance.'

I waved and left, feeling slightly deflated. We were both tourists.

The walking got very hard after that, especially once the green tropical trees turned back into dry gorse and the terrain left me exposed to the hot sun. There were some dramatic coves and beaches, but I could not spare even a moment to go down and explore them. I had to make Porthcurno by nightfall. I didn't have the 'torch' that was on the list. I had imagined I was to set fire to a wooden stick with a cloth at the end soaked in lighter fluid. No one told me that torch in English meant flashlight in American.

Staggering along, it all began to be too much for me. What was I doing on this insane coastal walk? My body was protesting strongly. I was out of my league here. No one knew where I was, except Graeme. If I fell and couldn't get up, I would die of exposure. Alone. Only thirty-five. Not yet a mid-career artist. I was dreaming of an air ambulance rescue, when I came over the crest of a hill and saw the secluded beach cove below that was Porthcurno. The sun was very low in the sky.

Chapter Three

The place where I was to stay was called Seaview House and I could see why. It was at the top of another hill, overlooking the cove, but the view was amazing. The sun had just set when I staggered the final fifty yards to the front door of Seaview House. When my host, James, opened the door, I could feel tears of relief in my eyes.

'You made it!' cried my host, a short, portly man, who patted me on the back. 'Just in time for the second act!'

'The what?'

'Just drop your pack over there. If you hurry, you'll make it. Here.' He held out two canvas bags to me. 'A blanket and a pillow.'

I strained to understand. Was James making me camp out in his garden?

'The play! Remember? You booked a ticket to the play tonight at the Minack Theatre! The open-air theatre carved into the rock? They're doing Twelfth Night. Now go! Don't want to miss this.'

'Wait. I can't possibly.'

'Oh, it's your only night here. You mustn't miss it! Take the bags. I do this for all my guests. You need these.'

'Blanket? Pillow?'

'The seats are made of stone, and it's quite cold out there on the cliffs.'

'In July?'

'Especially in July!'

This was the last thing I wanted to do right now.

'Couldn't I just stay here and have a bath?'

He shook his head and laughed, very much like the cab driver. A kind of snorting sound of hilarity.

'Off you go. It's just at the bottom of the hill.'

Yes, dear reader, he was sending me on another walk.

I took the bags and stumbled back down the hill. He was right. It was a once in a lifetime opportunity. Carrying the torch that he so kindly provided, I walked a further twenty minutes until I came to the Minack Theatre, which was indeed a theatre carved out of the rock cliff, overlooking the ocean.

Every seat had a perfect view of the stage. Beyond it was a moonlit sea. The setting was astonishing. I could hardly pay attention to the play. The stars were looking down from a velvety black sky and it was like I was at the edge of the world, looking out at the great beyond. All I could think about was how small we were compared to this ocean, this night sky and everything in it.

My host was right. This was a profoundly unique experience, not to be missed. It wasn't often possible to sit out here either. I've since learned there are heavy winds and rain the rest of the year. July and August were freezing at night, but the other months were worse. It astonished me that a group of thespians were able to perform at all under these conditions.

The blanket prevented hypothermia. The pillow was a welcome treat and a true kindness. Shakespeare in a Cornish accent was unintelligible, and unforgettable. And then my cell phone rang. I had forgotten to turn it off. I grabbed my pillow and blanket and ran out of the theatre with my phone.

'Not a good time, Graeme.'

'Grant. It's Bill.'

'Bill? Bill from school, Bill?'

'Yes. That Bill.' There was not the usual good humour in Bill's voice. 'You didn't answer your emails.'

We were supposed to answer all emails within 24 hours, but to tell the truth, I was kind of busy and hadn't even thought of checking email. The school was over for the summer, at least as far as I was concerned. This was annoying.

'I'm hiking. In England.'

There was a withering sigh.

'Well, Grant, there's a problem. A big problem.'

'Oh?'

'It's your grades. You've entered them incorrectly. Again. We can't access them. You'll need to come back and re-enter them. Immediately.'

I laughed. 'I'm halfway around the world at the moment. Couldn't it wait till I get back?'

'I'm afraid not. Parents are complaining. It's put us in a very embarrassing position.'

'Gee. Well. I'm so sorry, Bill. Really. But, man. I just can't see how I can do anything about it from here. I'm coming back next week. I'll come right–'

'Are your grades in your grade book? In your file drawer? Could we access them there?'

I thought of all the scribbling in my grade book. The crossed-out numbers. The missing assignments. The creative math.

'No. No. That won't work. I'm the only one who can read that gradebook.'

More heavy sighs. 'You've put me in a real bind here, Grant.'

'I'm sorry. I can't just leave now. It's not... possible. I promise to take care of it when I get back. I'll be back in a week.'

There was a very uncomfortable few seconds of silence.

'Never mind then, Grant. We'll just have to think of something else.'

Why didn't he just give everyone 'A's, I wondered. But then, the A+ and A- grades carried a great deal of weight with students and parents. He couldn't give those randomly.

'I'm sorry, Bill. I'll fix it. I promise. Just as soon as I get back.'

'No, you won't. Do you know why? Because you won't have a job when you get back.'

I stood there with the phone in my hand, the blanket draped around my shoulders. People flowed out of the theatre. A woman wearing a bulky blue coat and a black fur hat came over and stood in front of me, her arms crossed. She had on thick mascara and red lipstick.

'You look a bit lost. Are you a Yank?'

'I am. And a bit lost is what I am right now. I could use a drink. Would you care to join me? Where's the pub around here?'

Another girl appeared by her side, looking me up and down, a blonde with a shaggy short coat.

'This is Jill and I'm Beth.'

'I'm Grant. Very pleased to meet you. Could I buy both of you a drink?'

'Come on then. This way.'

'Thank you, ladies. I'm a long way from home. California.'

They both stopped walking and turned around to stare at me. 'What you doin' here, then?'

'I'm on a walking holiday. Doing the coastal walk.' I looked down at my poor feet, which thankfully, were too cold to have any more feeling to them.

'You left California weather for this?'

'Yes, I did. It's lovely here. Where are you two from? I can understand what you're saying, so you can't be from around here.'

They both laughed together in a charming unison. Beth spoke up as we walked along.

'We came from London to get summer work. We're at the Logan Rock Inn, cleaning rooms. It's not far from here. We had a night off, so we came over to see the show.'

When we arrived at the pub, it was full of people. What surprised me was the sight of families here, with little kids. There was a warm fire going, lots of laughter, and a menu that included milkshakes. Jill and Beth introduced me to the local brews: Towans, Lushingtons and Porthleven Pale Ale. For the rest of the evening, I let the beer blank out my mind.

Graeme called around eleven, to see if I was still alive. I was quite pleased to tell him that not only had I made the fourteen miles and seen the play, but I was out with two lovely ladies enjoying the evening. I was living large in Porthcurno!

'Well done. Don't stay out too late, you have another long day tomorrow. Fifteen miles to St Just.'

'Fifteen?'

'Yes.'

I gripped my glass. I thought the first day was going to be the worst. That detail must have escaped me.

'Brilliant.' I was baring my teeth in a smile at Beth, trying to be Full English about it.

'If you'd rather take a day off, you can always take the–.'

I hung up.

Chapter Four

The next day my feet were shattered. There was a gentle knock at the door and my host, James, placed a jar of Brave Soldier foot ointment in my hand and curled my fingers around it. I was becoming very fond of James. These little extra touches– the pillow, blanket, foot ointment, felt personal, like he was anticipating my every need. He also had a passing resemblance to Mr Carson, of Downton Abbey. While some part of me was appalled at the idea of having a servant, another part of me was enjoying the hell out of it. I could get used to James, making my life smooth, but I knew very well I had to push on to the next place.

I chose a sensible breakfast this time: two eggs over easy, toast and coffee. Saying my farewells, I shook James' hand, gazed into his kind blue eyes, and tried not to weep with gratitude. There was an impulse to tip him, but I remembered the English frowned on that. Never mind. James and his Seaview House would get five stars in my Trip Adviser review.

The trail hugged the coast now, and the views of the rocks and formations were stunning. There wasn't even a gorse bush in sight now, it was just me, the path, the sea, and the cliffs. It was a stark kind of beauty. I had to watch my step. The sun beat down on me. I slathered on the sun cream and tried to address my future. What future? I had just been fired, sacked as they say here, and that's what it felt like. Thrown out like a sack of garbage. Was it my fault that the grading system was so complicated? Could I help it if I wasn't around in the summer? What on earth would I do without a job? My savings were gone. All I had was the cash in my wallet. There were no teaching jobs I could apply for at this time of year.

In the depths of my despair, I was distracted by the views of the sea. It was there before me, spectacular and calming. You could see to the horizon, where the sea met the sky. The colours kept changing. The water would be aquamarine one minute, become turquoise, and then morph again and turn a deep blue. In every direction, there was nothing but a wide expanse. Sort of like my life, come to think of it.

The trail grew lonelier, even more existential. Before this point, I had seen the occasional walker, sometimes with a dog, but not anymore. It was just me, hugging the edge of the cliffs, at the end of the world. I was near a place called 'Land's End.' Were they kidding? It could have been called 'End of My Rope,' or 'End of My Tether,' since we're doing the Full English. One misstep and I could fall to my death in the vast Atlantic Ocean and not even Graeme would know I was gone. When I didn't answer his call tonight, he would just write me up as another dumb American who didn't take the bus.

I didn't tell anyone I was going hiking in Cornwall–not my therapist, Trent, not my sometimes girlfriend, Charon (yes, that's her real name), not Kevin (my long-time friend and surf buddy), not Bill (my boss) and certainly not my family. Why? Why did I choose not to tell anyone I was hiking by myself, halfway around the world?

If I were on the couch asking this question of Trent, I know just what he'd say. Trent would ask me what I think it means. Since I have to do all the work in this relationship, I'd say, 'It means I feel the need to escape my life. To run and hide, to the other side of the earth.' A minute later, he would reply, 'And why is that?' I'd then give Trent my thoughtful insights. 'I want to get away from my job because I hate it. I want to get away from my family because they hate me. I want to get away from Charon, because she wants to ferry me across the river of death to a marriage I do not want. Not with her. Not with anyone. And I want to get away from my friend Kevin because his adventures are way better than mine. By this point, my time would be up, Trent would close his notebook and hold the door open for me. That'd be it until our next session. Only now there would be no next session because I'd either die on this trip or come back unemployed and be unable to afford therapy.

Cornwall had sounded adventurous. Daring. But now I knew Graeme was right. I didn't prepare properly for it. I was probably going to die. I might have been saved if I had the whistle around my neck that was on the list. I would have been blowing on the thing for all I was worth as I fell down the cliff. Someone might have heard it and at least been able to find my dead body somewhere down there, but no, I've totally fucked this up. This whole trip. This little life of mine.

Was my life comparable to this vast expanse in front of me? Was it a whole lot of nothing? Or was it an endless possibility? Was I master of my fate or did a silly computer error and bad timing get me fired and make me penniless at age thirty-five, or worse, forty? One thing was for sure. Having no future source of income was making me very jittery. I needed a coffee.

I pulled out the map and discovered that Land's End was just ahead. I'd be able to get coffee and some lunch there too. I could feel a few coins in my pocket. Hopefully, it wouldn't be overpriced, even if it was the only place for miles. The trail took me to a huge 'car park' or, as we call it in America, a 'parking lot.' There was a hotel (painted white), and a marketplace (also painted white) where white people were selling white people's food—items of little nutritional value that were either salty or sweet. There was ice cream, muffins, brownies, sausages, burgers, chips (French Fries in America), popcorn and something called 'candy floss' which I realised was 'cotton candy' in America. I managed to find something resembling coffee.

They also sold snow globes of lighthouses, statues of animals, and nautical items and there were loads of T-shirts. The Land's End logo was everywhere, but I was confused about what it represented. I thought Land's End was a mail-order company in the States that sold leisurewear. Here it seemed to represent a very specific lighthouse on a rock.

I really couldn't find anything appetising in the market, so I walked back to the trail to see what the tourists were taking pictures of. It was the lighthouse on a rock. I was told by one of the tourists, that this was the famous Land's End lighthouse, called Longships, and beyond it were the Isles of Scilly, pronounced 'silly.' Things are not what they appear to be in print here, but that's England for you. These were the most western parts of England and Cornwall. I took a picture, just to be sociable.

At this point, I was hungry, dog tired, and close to having a stroke. It was very hot. I went back to the Land's End parking lot, trying to gather the courage to buy a burger, when a bus rolled up. The bus I had heard so much about from Graeme. It was a double-decker, partially open on top! The number seven. Was this a sign? Was this bus here to tempt me into doing the thing I vowed I would not do? The door swished open before me like the promise of relief. I stepped up, telling myself I was just going to speak to the driver. Ask one question. That's all.

'Does this bus go to St Just?'

'Yes.'

'How much?' That's two questions.

'Two quid.'

I fished in my pocket for the biggest, fattest piece of change in England and slapped it on the little business counter in front of the driver. He took it and pushed a button. The machine spat out a paper ticket and I took it. The deal was done. I had danced with the devil and now I was going to put my feet up and enjoy the ride. I climbed the stairs and sat down under the shade of the partial covering and gazed out at the scenery. I felt regal. Lord of all I could see. The bus hissed and growled like a huge beast as it pulled out of the lot, and everyone got out of its way. The wind ruffled my hair and there was a smile on my face. For a mere two pounds, I'd left my troubles behind me in the parking lot.

The bus rambled along twisty roads and green hills. The stone walls divided farms that had been around for millennia. The trip took twenty-six minutes and saved me about six hours of walking. We pulled into St Just, a town of honey-coloured stone buildings, no trees in sight, at one-thirty. I was refreshed by the ride and ready to forage for food in this lovely place.

There wasn't much in St Just, except a stone church and a few stone buildings, but happily, there was a bookstore called The Cookbook, which was also a café. I've always loved the idea of combining a bookstore and café. A sign in the window, lettered by hand, announced a soup and salad deal and 'The Best Chocolate Cake in England.' I stood there on the street a moment and then laughed out loud. Right. OK, fine. You got me. I will investigate this claim too.

The soup was carrot and coriander. I also had the house salad and a slice of the chocolate cake with a large glass of water. The cake was excellent. The frosting had just the right amount of sugar and butter. My taste buds were torn with loyalty to the previous best chocolate cake. I decided it was a draw. They both had a good claim to the title.

I browsed around looking at the books. There were a lot of out-of-date cookbooks, romance novels and tourist books about Cornwall. I was glad I wasn't tempted. It was becoming painfully obvious that I was getting poorer by the day. I was running out of money and that was going to be very embarrassing when I tried to use my bank card at a cash machine.

The woman who served me spoke something like English. Her name was Barbara, and she was both the cook and owner of the shop. I was the only customer, so I imagined business must be very slow in the winter. The soup and salad were delicious. The chocolate cake, however, was out of this world! Moist. Rich. Chocolatey. The frosting thick and sweet, not too buttery. It was even better than the last one. I asked her how there could be two best chocolate cakes in England, and she just smiled and shrugged. 'We like our cake here.' She told me that in England they call a person's mouth a 'cake hole.' This cracked me up.

On my way out, I tried to interest her in buying my pirate book, but she declined gracefully. She already had plenty of books about pirates. I asked her about the name of the town, and the Saint associated with the church. She said Saint Just was a martyr who was drowned in Trieste, Italy, for being a Christian in the year 293. And on that cheerful note, I headed out of St Just, reminded that it was good to be alive, and that I was in a country that believed in cake. I was now actually halfway through my Cornwall Adventure. Tomorrow would be an easy six-mile walk to Zennor, where I would spend the night and then walk the final six miles to St Ives.

The road leading out of town had low stone walls on both sides. Cows were chewing their cud and watched me as I walked. They came over to the wall to get a better look. We studied each other. I love cows. Unlike students, they look like they're paying attention when you talk to them. They were gorgeous. Red and brown and white. Long eyelashes. Big dopy eyes. There were horses too. With long tails and burly legs.

I stopped to look at my map. This was the road to Boswedden House, the guesthouse on a farm. It was another sunny day, though the winds were strong and bracing. I think the rest on the bus did me good. I was feeling fine as I walked along enjoying the clean air. It was four o'clock when I came to the big white house with two chimneys. I could see a woman hanging sheets on a clothesline and hippies were dancing on the front lawn.

Shaken by the incongruous sight, I drew nearer to investigate. There were indeed Bongo drums. Tie-dye shirts. Baggy pants. Dreadlocks. Hippies. They were swinging their bodies and shaking tambourines. I stood there watching a moment, wondering what sort of ritual this was, when a barefoot man, otherwise formally dressed, came out of the house holding a tray with drinks, which he set down on the lawn before the bongo player. He turned, saw me, and smiled, his blondish curly hair blowing in the wind. Adjusting his black horn-rimmed glasses, he addressed me.

'May I help you, Sir?'

'I'm Grant Decker.'

'Oh! Mr Decker! We weren't expecting you this early. Did you take the bus?'

Must everyone know my business?

'Part of the way, yes.' I smiled.

'Well, your room is ready if you want to take your things up.'

'That would be great. Thanks.'

'My name's Nigel. I don't wear shoes.'

'So I see.'

'I never could stand them,' he said, then turned to lead me through the front door of the grand house.

'Very nice,' I said as we entered. I wondered if I should remove my shoes like Nigel, but there were no other empty shoes scattered at the entrance, so I didn't.

'I live here with my wife and daughter.' He climbed the stairs and I followed. I couldn't help staring at his feet. They looked like hairy shoes. It was as if the lower half of him was a hobbit and the top half, was a Duke, or an Earl. At the top of the stairs, we turned left, and he opened the door to a spacious room with twin beds. The interior design style of the room was a time capsule of England in the 1940s. Green velvet bed covers, floral chintz curtains, Edwardian bedside tables, Chinese ceramic lamps with indigo designs and an overstuffed reading chair in the corner by the window, upholstered to match the curtains.

I set my things down on the floor and was invited to examine the white-tiled bathroom off the bedroom. The plumbing looked modern which meant a hot shower. I nodded, more than happy.

The Barefoot Nigel gave me a key and told me breakfast was between seven and ten in the breakfast room. I asked if I might have poached eggs and he said yes, of course. This man who had been visited by time-travelling hippies, seemed able to handle anything. I had faith in him. He waved and went off, I assume, to attend to the bongo players.

The shower was hot. Instantly! It felt luxurious. After warming my tired muscles, I laid out on the bed and resumed my pirate studies. Blackbeard was causing a great deal of trouble in the Caribbean and along the coast of America, becoming a menace to the new American economy. While in England, Captain Kidd was disrupting trade routes. There were even women pirates, Anne Bonny and Mary Read, pretending to be men. Anarchy everywhere! Pirates were becoming a world economic problem and governments were now paying huge sums to get rid of them. They didn't just want the pirates taken out of the game, they wanted to make an example of them—their dead bodies swaying in the wind, hung in cages, pecked at by birds. At the end of the eighteenth century, quite a lot of the fun had been taken out of the job. The Golden Age of Pirates was coming to an end when my phone rang.

Chapter Five

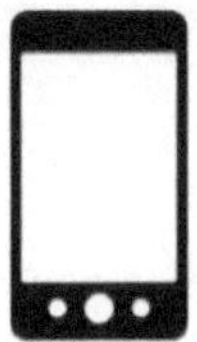

'Hello?'

'Greetings, Mr Decker. Are you in St Just?'

'Indeed, I am, Graeme. How are you?'

'Oh, I'm quite well. How are you, Sir?'

'Excellent! Couldn't be better.'

'Not sore?'

'Well, a bit. But I'll live.'

'Good. You should have a fairly easy time of it from here on. Just six miles a day. I expect you'll get into Zennor tomorrow afternoon sometime.'

'Easy peasy.' I laughed. 'You say that here, don't you?'

'Uh, yes. Now. I won't ring you on your mobile tomorrow night. There's no Internet there.'

'Wha–?'

'I've asked your hostess, Sue, to call me on her landline if you don't turn up by six o'clock.'

'She won't mind?'

'Not a bit. We've done this before. She's got a seventeenth-century cottage and likes to keep it that way. The cottage is a mile or so inland from the church at Zennor. It's on the map.'

'No Internet at all then?'

'Is that a problem?'

'Not for me, no.' I didn't have to worry about those pesky work emails anymore.

'Good. It's a lovely place. I'm sure you'll enjoy it. Very quiet.'

'Where might I get some dinner?'

'There's a pub in Zennor. Oh, and a youth hostel, where they also serve meals. Just drop your things at the cottage and head on into town after that. You'll need to bring your torch for the walk back.'

'I don't have a torch, Graeme.'

'It was on the list.'

'I'll get to the cottage before dark.'

'Right then. Cheerio.'

I hung up and realised it was actually pretty nice to be thought of daily like this. Graeme was the only one checking in on me. True, he was the only one who knew I was here, but still, no one else was bothering to check if I was alive or dead. To be fair, it could have been my fault. I had pre-empted my mother calling by talking to her just before I left. We arranged to talk twice a month, no more. And Charon, well... we'd argued. I was trying to work out the same deal with her. A call every two weeks. No more. She thought that unreasonable and hung up on me. That was a week ago and I got the feeling she was going to hold out longer. Maybe forever. She was pretty mad. But honestly, I didn't miss Charon. We always ran out of things to talk about. Not that Graeme and I were what you'd call close, but it was...well...lovely to know that someone cared if I lived or died daily. Even if it wasn't personal, I imagined it might be very nice if it was.

I drifted off to sleep in my comfortable room and was soon dreaming of the pirate life during the Golden Age—a life of freedom, adventure, and a little harmless booty on the side. It was as if the land of Cornwall itself, contained pirate souls that snaked up from the soil and seeped into my brain, playing out different versions of who I might be. Pirate Grant! Captain Decker! Greybeard! When I woke up I was famished.

Having forgotten all about dinner the previous night, I was now looking forward to a big breakfast. I got my things together, got dressed and went downstairs.

The breakfast room had high ceilings, pale green swagged curtains and a dozen small tables with white linen tablecloths, a cut glass vase filled with wildflowers. The Barefoot Nigel served me a couple of perfect poached eggs on toast, four sausages, hash browns and orange juice. The coffee was especially good. Rich. Full-bodied. I was feeling well-rested. Surprisingly calm.

And there was Nigel, smiling back at me. He appeared to be at peace with himself as he stood there in his white shirt, black waistcoat, and trousers, standing on an oriental rug, in his bare feet. His wife, who was in the kitchen doing the cooking, peeked out the service window and waved. His little girl was carrying salt and pepper shakers to each table. She was about six and had Nigel's blond curly hair. I noticed she had no trouble wearing shoes. Shiny black leather ones, with frilly socks.

After my breakfast, I said my farewells to the Barefoot Nigel and his family and was off to the coast path again, this time headed for Zennor! What a name! I gave it a quick look on my phone and discovered that Zennor may have been the place named for one of the Cornish saints, Saint Senara. Legend had it that she was a Breton princess, the wife of a Breton king who, when she became pregnant, was accused of adultery by her husband and thrown into the sea in a barrel. She was visited by an angel and gave birth to her son on the waves. He later became Saint Budoc of Ireland. She and her son were washed up on the Cornish coast at the place now called Zennor and a church was built there in her honour, though there were lingering doubts about her honour. Some believed she did commit adultery and got what was coming to her.

As I walked along the coast path, the landscape started taking on eery shapes in my imagination. There were giants! Kings! Queens! Pirates! Saints in barrels! Cornwall had set all this in motion, with a rich mix of history, archaeology, myth, legend, and fairy tale. To an American like me, this was all so different, so exotic. Here there were mine shafts, stone circles, and burial mounds. A bit further up the coast were the ruins of Tintagel Castle, the birthplace of the man thought to be the real King Arthur! I stopped now and then to take pictures, sketch, and dream.

I had ancestral roots in this part of the world, though no one in my family had been back here since I was born. My father's family came from Wales and Scotland. My mother came from Germany. I was the usual American mix of things. The longer I was here, however, the more certain I became of a feeling that I belonged here. My body felt at home in this world. I'd seen other people with hair that curled the same way mine did, with hands and noses and ears that looked like mine too.

As I walked on, I noticed the gorse was back. Now there were wildflowers and heather. The trail hugged the cliffs as before. There were spectacular views of beautiful beaches and coves dotted with intriguing caves and arches. The emerald waters of these coves dazzled my eyes. The Pacific Ocean was nothing like this. The light was different, as were the colours of the sea. I found a nice flat rock on which to perch, an idyllic view before me. I removed my shirt and sunned myself like a lizard.

Chapter Six

Maybe being fired was not the worst thing that could happen to me. I knew I wasn't happy as a teacher. It was an uneasy compromise between doing what my family expected of me and what I wanted to do. Every year I sank further into a feeling of numbness, like I was a fraud, not pleasing anyone.

To apply for another teaching job seemed pointless. Why should I repeat this farce? Fear of poverty, that's why. Yeah. There was that. Teaching was the only thing I knew how to do for money. And I wasn't the worst teacher in the world. My sheer enthusiasm for art was genuine and art kids felt that. We shared a bond, but I could feel their mild disgust that I was a teacher, after all, just like the other teachers. Failures.

I told myself, every year, that school holidays and summer would be my time to make art, but you have to make a lot of photographs to get anything good. Robert Frank was a photographer I taught in my classes. He shot 27,000 pictures for his book 'The Americans,' but included only 83 of them. A Guggenheim Fellowship in 1955 allowed him to spend a year taking those pictures and driving 10,000 miles to find them. He took his wife and two children with him. They mostly lived in his car. He needed time and the freedom to do this work. He was striving for art, and as the recipient of that grant, he was expected to achieve it. He took astonishing artistic risks, making photographs that were not like anything ever done before. His work was pioneering, and he forever changed the way the world saw photography.

You don't set out on the path of becoming an artist by becoming a teacher. Teaching demands an entirely different skill set. It is a profession that seeks to avoid risk. Schools do not handle failure well, trying to avoid it at all costs. It promotes competition over collaboration. It has little to do with authenticity and is a training ground for those seeking the approval of groups. School sapped my energies while distancing me from any kind of art life.

Teachers are an entirely different tribe than artists. Even children are wise to this charade. An art teacher claiming to know what it meant to be an artist seemed like someone either crazy or seriously deluded. It was sort of like taking students to a zoo to learn about lions. What could you know about lions in that context? Or butterflies pinned to a board? Schools present art and artists in the most abstract distanced way. You got trite little lesson plans with a Van Gogh romanticism sufficiently packaged to make art look, at best, like a colourful representation of feeling and, at worst, like the activity of mental illness. It was positioned in the school landscape to provide stress relief for students and assure parents that their child would never choose it as a serious career. Why had I spent so many years of my life struggling against this soul-killing environment?

I scanned the flat calm of the sea. Sometimes a seal would pop its head up to look around and then dive under again. This brought to mind the story of the sealskin mother. A female seal takes off her seal skin one night to dance around a fire on an island with other seals on a certain magical night. A fisherman watches her from behind a bush and steals her seal skin. He falls in love with her and convinces her to marry him, promising to give her back her seal skin in seven years. She marries him and has a child, but she continues to grow weak without her seal skin. After seven years the fisherman refuses to return the skin, knowing he will lose her to the sea. One day, their son finds the sealskin and brings it to her. She puts it on and is restored to her seal form. She explains to the boy she must go back to the sea or perish. She promises that she will always come to the shore by the cottage if the boy calls for her. He grows up as a fisherman, like his father, understanding his connection to the sea, which provides him with food. He continues to see his mother in the ocean.

I'd always liked this story. Now it seemed especially meaningful. As a teacher, I felt like a creature of the sea trying to live on land. It was making me weaker and weaker to be there. I had to live in the sea, somehow, to breathe. It was going to be uncomfortable, conflicting even, to leave, but now that decision had been made for me. I was out, and it was up to me to go in the direction of where I belonged. It would probably be very scary and there was a lot to learn, but it was the only way to be authentic, and accept who I was. It was better for me to fail at being a photographer than succeed in being a photography teacher.

Stretching my arms up to the sky, I knew it was time to move. I wasn't going to be a teacher anymore. That alone felt powerful. Hopeful. It would be a very hard conversation to have with my family, but it was the right thing to do. The risk of losing their love, which was at the heart of my fear, was worth what I would gain, which was self-respect. If I only got one life, I knew I had to choose the life that was mine. Happiness could only come if I understood my purpose and sought out my destiny. As I walked down the path I felt lighter. I didn't know what was ahead of me. I was going to have to try things and fail. There was no security in my future and no guarantees. But I knew I'd not only survive failure, but I'd also learn from it. Freedom was what I was after, like the pirates, and I needed to know what that felt like.

Consulting the map, repeatedly, I was finally able to find the cottage where I would be staying near Zennor. Tucked behind a stone wall was a garden wrapped around a stone house that was built to stand centuries of wind. My eyes roamed over it taking in the details of the thick walls, the small windows, the mature trees around it and the two curious white cats that sat on the grass judging me with slant eyes. I bent over and held out my hand, the appropriate, prostrate position for introducing myself to cats. One meowed, the other was utterly silent but wandered over, none too eager, a kind of tolerant acceptance of my gesture. Soon both were following me to the door which was at the back of the house.

After I knocked, the wide blue door opened. A round sunburned face smiled back at me with dark eyes and hair streaked with gold. I introduced myself, though she was expecting me. This was Sue. Her house was like a living museum of the seventeenth century. She had a spinning wheel in one corner, an enormous open fireplace with a wood stove, pots and kettles and dried plants hanging from the low, wood-beamed ceiling. A long oak table with benches had reeds on it, she was making her baskets. I didn't see one modern thing. Her clothing was simply cut in earth tones. Sue was living in another time and looked perfectly at home with herself.

'Your room is up the stairs to the right. There is a tub and shower to the left. Why don't you drop your pack up there and you can grab some dinner in town? I'll have breakfast ready for you in the morning.'

'Great. Thanks.'

I trudged up the stairs and was delighted to see bookshelves built into every nook. There were good books, from what I could see. Literary books. Art and photography books. I liked Sue already. The room was tiny but there was a comfortable looking bed and the smell of hay on the sheets. A small window framed a view that swept down the hill, over a patchwork of farms to the rocky coastline and out to sea.

Sue stood at the door to my room.

'The youth hostel has surprisingly good food. They specialise in soups.' Her voice woke me from my daydream. I set down my knapsack and took out my wallet, slipped it into my pocket and followed her down the stairs.

'Is it easy to find?'

'Just across from the church. You can't miss it. And don't forget to check out the mermaid chair.'

'The what?'

'The mermaid chair. In the church. It's 800 years old. Worth a look. It's in the very back.'

'OK. Thanks.'

I smiled and ducked out the low-slung door, walking back out through the garden. After bowing to the cats, I went out the back gate and returned to the trail leading to Zennor. It was only a mile to the town.

Before long I saw the squared-off tower of St Senara. The sun was streaming through grey clouds, landing on the centuries-old structure like a beacon. The church, at the centre of the town, was surrounded by a few cottages, the pub, and the youth hostel. There seemed to be no one around. It was dead quiet.

I walked up the steps to the gothic entry and went through the door. Standing still for a moment, to let my eyes adjust, I took off my hat. There was the musty smell of earth and mildew, a hint of candle wax. The stone inside was bone coloured and appeared to be older than the rest of the building. It was a small chapel. The curved wood ceiling above made it feel closed in. There were rows of stone arches and one narrow stained-glass window near the altar. The benches were of dark wood and had crude decorative carvings along the aisle. The swirling lines reminded me of waves. I looked around for anything that might be called a chair and finally saw it, by the baptismal font. The short bench had a flat cushion, decorated with five colourful fish. A mermaid with long hair trailing down her arms and a round belly was carved into the side of the dark wood chair. She was holding up a disc and a comb. Parts of her face were gouged out.

What did a mermaid have to do with Saint Senara, the unfortunate woman thrown into the sea in a barrel for imagined infidelity? It certainly looked old, with a kind of primitive, almost childlike, rendering of this mythical creature. Trailing my finger over the rough surface of the carving, I got a very strange feeling. There was more to this story. Parts missing, like the face. The saint and the mermaid both came from the sea. They both seemed to be pregnant, but what was this disc? And what happened to her face?

After some time standing there, my stomach growled, and I decided to get some dinner before the sun went down. The youth hostel was set back from the road, down a slight hill in a clean white building that looked new but had the proportions of an old barn. There were some picnic tables outside. A few people were sitting on benches with ice cream, others with soup and bread. The soup smelled fabulous.

Chapter Seven

There were high ceilings. As I came to the wood counter, a woman wearing a long white apron came out of the kitchen. She was strikingly beautiful. Long wavy red hair swayed behind her as she walked. She smiled and looked at me with the kindest green eyes I'd ever seen.

'Dydh da,' she said.

I just smiled like a fool and stared at her, trying to memorise her face.

She crossed her arms and tilted her head, still smiling, as if trying to figure me out.

I pointed to myself.

'Ignorant American. No idea what you just said. My name's Grant.'

'Ah. Well, dydh da is Cornish for hello. Try it. Dydh da.'

'Did da.'

'Dydh da. So, what can I get for you, Grant?'

'Your name. I'd like to learn your name.'

She put her hands on her hips and narrowed her eyes.

'It's Nara. And I'm expected to take your order.'

'Right. Well, thank you, Nara. What's the soup today?'

'Butternut squash.'

'I'll have that.'

'Anything to drink?'

'Can I get a latte?'

'Of course.'

'And I don't suppose you have chocolate cake...'

'Best chocolate cake in England,' she said, without irony.

'Oh, I must have that then.' She wrote it up, gave me the total and I paid her. But I didn't want her to leave. 'Are you named for Saint Senara?'

'My mother liked the name.'

She turned and ducked into the kitchen. Her long hair swung back and forth, ending just below her trim waist.

When she came back with a tray of food she asked me where I wanted to eat. I glanced around and went to a table near the counter, pulling out a chair. She placed the tray in front of me.

'I don't mean to rush you, but we close in fifteen minutes.'

'In that case, there is something I must tell you.'

She tilted her head and blinked.

'Go on then.'

'I'm a photographer and... well... I'm very interested in the mermaid legend. The chair. After you're done here, might I buy you a drink and ask you a few questions about it?'

She cleared her throat.

'I'm not a tour guide.'

'No. I'm sorry. I realise that. I just thought...well, you were so kind, and I thought you might help me out. Plesya?' Thank God I remembered that one Cornish word. The word for please.

She raised her eyebrows. A slow smile came to her lips.

'I'll meet you in the church cemetery in twenty minutes.'

Chapter Eight

Twenty minutes was just enough time to thoroughly enjoy the delicious soup, coffee, and cake. And yes, it was the best chocolate cake in England. Even better than the other best chocolate cakes I had in Cornwall. Of course, I could very well be hopelessly biased at this point. I was in love or bewitched or bamboozled, but I didn't care. I was going to see her again and that's all that mattered.

When I came to the church cemetery, I was amazed at how large it was. Some of the grave markers were huge. Towering Celtic crosses, stone slabs that looked like low beds surrounded by deep green grass. The dates on the graves were mostly nineteenth century. I imagined men wearing stovepipe hats with stiff collars and women with gloved hands, holding elaborate fans, in high waist dresses. They were all bones now, slumbering under grey stone comforters.

Around the back of the church, I spotted Nara, her hair around her shoulders like a silky red cloak. She was no longer wearing the apron but was in a blue shirt, jeans, and sandals. Her hands were in her pockets. She waved and then strolled over to meet me as I walked toward her.

'Dydh da,' I said, enormously relieved to see her.

There was that smile again. Her green eyes curious. Interested. At least I hoped so.

'You've seen the chair then?' she asked.

'Yes. The mermaid looks pregnant. Why is that? And what is the disc she holds? And the comb?'

She started walking along the path in an ambling way and I walked too, keeping pace with her.

'The disc is a mirror. And together with the comb, it symbolises vanity. The mermaid is often portrayed this way in art. Vain, with dubious powers. The people who made that chair, almost a thousand years ago, lived at a time when Christianity was just starting to be established, competing with the old religions, with

69

superstitions, myths, and legends. They made the mermaid look pregnant to merge Saint Senara's story with the mermaid's story. Both were women who came from the sea and survived tragedies.

'It looks like the face of the mermaid has been damaged.'

'Vandalism. A long time ago. In both the legend of the mermaid and Saint Senara's story, the sympathy is not with the woman. The people of the town of Zennor lost one of their own to the mermaid and the sea. And not everyone believed that the mermaid, or even Saint Senara, was innocent.'

'They doubted her sainthood?'

Nara crossed her arms and tilted her head again. It felt like she was stepping away from me.

'The Cornish people are rather distrusting of authority. They believe in their own stories and legends over those of the Church or the government. Maybe I better tell you the whole mermaid story. But not here. Come with me.'

She led the way, and as we went out of the churchyard toward the sea, every cell in my body was buzzing. Something powerful was happening. I wondered if she felt it too. I wanted to know this woman. Deeply. Our footsteps crunched the gravel as we followed the twists and turns of the path, first up a steep hill and then down to the edge of a cliff, where we stopped. There was a view of an idyllic cove hundreds of feet below us, reflecting the golden light of the setting sun. We sat down on a smooth black rock. The breeze was blowing Nara's hair straight out behind her, and she looked like a mermaid herself. Strong, beautiful, otherworldly.

'Mermaids like to sing,' she said, her voice as smooth and warm as honey. 'Their song is beautiful, hypnotic. It casts a spell. There's a long tradition of stories about sailors being lured to their deaths at sea by the songs of mermaids. The Zennor Mermaid came out of the sea because she was drawn to the singing of humans, at Saint Senara's Church on Sunday mornings. She came to the church one day, as a human, and began to sing with them. One of the singers was the son of the vicar. He had a lovely singing voice too.'

'When the singing was over, the beautiful woman left the church without speaking a word. No one knew her name or where she came from. She became a regular, coming each Sunday to sing with the congregation. One day, after the singing was over, the vicar's son followed her down the path to this very cove, and to his surprise, she changed form. Her legs merged to form a fishtail and she swam away. The next Sunday, he followed her to the cove again and proclaimed his love for her. She told him she loved him too but couldn't live on land as a human. Her powers only let her visit for a short time. She did, however, have the power to change him into a merman, but he could never live on land again.'

'So, he would have to change for her.'

'Yes.'

'What happened?'

'He agreed and before long they had a little family. People still claim to see them in the cove, frolicking in the sea with their mer children.'

'A happy ending then.'

'For the mermaid and the vicar's son, yes. But the villagers saw it differently. They told the story as a cautionary tale of sin and seduction and made Saint Senara a similar character in her story. To them, she was not a saint, but guilty of violating her marriage vows because she was beautiful and vain. They took her husband's view of the truth, that she was unfaithful. Not hers.

The villagers also saw the mermaid as being beautiful and vain, a sinner who lured the vicar's son away from the church and his own species.'

'So, they hacked at her face on the chair?'

'Most vandalism is the product of shame and fear. Over time, many faces have been erased from churches, leaving only certain kinds of faces behind. The saints and angels. The goblins and demons that guarded churches have been destroyed by those who feared them and their difference.'

'Why wasn't the mermaid erased?'

'The fishermen of Zennor saw the mermaid as a symbol of Christ because she crossed boundaries and existed in two worlds, like a man born of heaven and earth.'

I watched Nara twirl her hair around her finger and opened my camera bag.

'May I please take your picture?'

She sighed heavily.

'I have to get going.'

'It won't take long. The light's going anyway. Can I just take a few shots?'

'Go on then.'

Nara stood up, put her hands in her pockets and turned her face toward the sun on the horizon. I snapped as many pictures as I could, desperate to capture something about her that I couldn't even name. The sun illuminated her deep green eyes, and, in that instant, I got my picture.

'You don't have time for that drink?'

I only heard her footsteps as I followed her down the path. By the time we got to the pub, it was dark, the light coming from the windows was warm and bright, voices could be heard, laughter. There was music drifting from the window. A fiddle and some singing.

'I can't stay,' she said, then held her hand out. 'It was nice to meet you, Grant.'

'Nara, thank you. You helped me understand some important things about the mermaid. It was so...good... to meet you.' We stood in silence for a moment, our eyes locked in longing and confusion. 'Could I get your phone number?' She stared at me. 'Or an email address? I could send you the pictures I took.'

She shook her head. Her eyes glistened for a moment, and then she turned and ran down the path. The darkness swallowed her up like the sea. And just like that, my beautiful mermaid was gone.

Chapter Nine

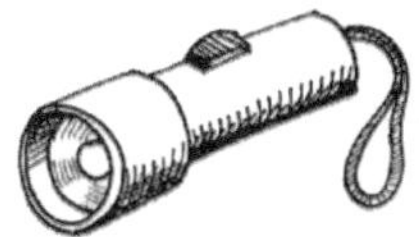

I found my way down the path in the twilight, went into the pub and ordered Cornish rum. But thoughts of Nara still plagued me, along with the strange tale of the Zennor mermaid. Turning my camera around, I scrolled through the pictures I'd taken of her. She was even more beautiful than I remembered, hauntingly so. Those sea-green eyes were looking back at me. It was as if she was seeing me in ways that I'd never been seen before.

The bartender loaned me a torch so I could find Sue's cottage in the dark. She'd left a lantern lit in the window for me. I found my room at the top of the stairs and slipped between the cold sheets of the downy bed, wondering how to see Nara again, but every time I came up with a plan, the obvious flaw in it emerged. She didn't want to see me.

This, the voice of reason said, was a one-sided silly crush I had on a beautiful woman who happened to fill some far-fetched dream I had. Even if, by some stretch of the imagination, she was interested in me, and we attempted a relationship, what exactly could I offer her? I was a foreigner, with no job. And I could just imagine what my family would make of it. Still, the other voice in me persisted. What if this is the woman I'm supposed to be with? I've never had this feeling before. This is something very special and I should pay attention to this. But the killjoy's voice answered again. She has a life here. You don't have a life, even in America, and you can't legally stay. Besides, she closed the door. She offered no way to contact her. That's a hard no.

I got up and went to the window. There was a gibbous moon, and I could see the faint outline of the long slope of grass extending to the sea. Near the water was a strange green light, slowly flashing on and off. I wondered if it was some sort of beacon. It must have been. After staring at it for a long time, I finally went back to bed and told myself to forget about Nara. She was a beautiful, kind woman who told me the story of the mermaid. That's all.

I dreamed that night of mermaids, half fish, half-human. And the other halves I'd heard about that day: Christ, the half-human, half God. Then there was the myth of our other half. Why did I believe so strongly that it was Nara?

When I woke the sky was grey. I carried my pack downstairs and could smell the pancakes Sue was serving up. There was syrup and strawberries, blackberries, eggs, sausage, and fresh coffee. I ate with enthusiasm, as we made small talk. Sue bustled about like a mother hen and seemed pleased to feed me. When I finally finished, there was nothing left to say. It was time for me to go. I put on my coat and stood there before Sue until I finally blurted out what was really on my mind.

'Do you know a woman in the village named Nara?'

She looked at me and crossed her muscular arms.

'Of course. I know everyone here.'

'Can you tell me a little about her?'

'What do you want to know?'

'Is she married?'

Sue's smile grew rueful.

'No.'

'Could you give me her phone number?'

'You better get going. There's a storm coming. You probably just have time to make it to St Ives.'

'A last name? Anything? Sue, I must see her again. Please.'

'You're on holiday, Mr Decker. You're not the first one to fall in love with Nara. You'll forget about her in a few days.'

'You don't understand...'

'Off you go. Don't take the coast path today. It's going to be a big storm and the coast path will be too dangerous. Take the inland path, you'll go through the fields, over farmland. You must watch the path carefully, because the cows sometimes tread over it, and you could lose it.'

'All right.'

I sighed.

'You have a compass?'

'I'll be fine. Eyes on the trail. Got it.'

She stared at me, then headed for the kitchen.

'Let me get you a compass.'

'No, no. I'll be fine, Sue. Really. You've been very kind. Breakfast was fabulous. Thank you so much.'

I raised my hand, like a presidential candidate, and was out the door, striding toward the gate. She came to the window, pushed it open and stuck her head through.

'Good luck!' she called.

Chapter Ten

The wind was picking up and I felt like Dorothy in the Wizard of Oz, trying to get home before the cyclone hit. If Cornwall had tumbleweeds, they would have rolled by ominously in this wind. Right now, I had to concentrate on getting to St Ives. It wasn't that far, only eight or ten miles of trail. I should have time to look around the town, have a nice dinner and in the morning, take the train back to London. My Cornwall adventure was nearing its end.

Every day had been sunny on my walking trip thus far, but today was a stark change. The sky was getting darker. The wind stronger.

Forceful gusts were swirling in the air. The trees were whipping their limbs around as if they were possessed by demons. The cows were hunkering down together for protection. Things were set for drama, and I had a nervous feeling in the pit of my stomach. The words, 'especially in July,' came back to me with Graeme's warnings about the changeable weather and I knew I was stunningly unprepared for what was coming.

As I walked on, I tried to comfort myself with thoughts of Nara bringing me the best chocolate cake in England. I played a film in my head of her telling me the story of the mermaid, her eyes gleaming, her soft voice carrying me into the story. I saw the vicar's son transforming into a merman because of his love for her, which, of course, made me imagine a conversion to a Cornish life. I'd give up being an American. Nara and I would bake bread together in a cottage in Zennor. I'd play spoons in the band at the local pub. There would be long walks in the sunset. The stars at night. That strange green light flashing on and off in the distance.

With each step, my hope of this fantasy life grew stronger until I stopped, so sure of this dream becoming a reality that I twirled around, throwing my hat up in the air like Mary Tyler Moore in the opening of her TV show in the sixties. I caught it with finesse and turned around just in time to see a man approaching from a distance, a group of farm buildings in the background. He was clearly a farmer, and I was on his land. He had, no doubt, seen me twirling around like a fool and had reason to be concerned. I stood there, holding my hat, and trying to think of some way to explain myself.

As he came closer, I saw he was not angry, just incredulous.

'What are you doing here? There's a big storm coming.' His face was weathered and wrinkled, his hat faded and worn. He wore tall wellies up to the knee, spattered with mud.

'Yes, yes, I know. I'm just on my way to St Ives.'

'Why don't you take the bus? It comes along that road.' He pointed over his shoulder.

I smiled. Lost tourists must worry them.

'Ran out of money!' I said, only half-joking.

He immediately dug in his pocket and produced coins, which he held out to me.

'Take these.'

I was horrified. This man was quite determined to get me on a bus. I held up both hands.

'No, thank you. Really. I'd rather walk. I need the exercise.'

He sighed and put the coins back in his pocket, shook his head and left, stomping back across the field, like he had an urgent appointment.

I resumed my walk. It was a point of pride. I had already taken the bloody bus once. I would at least finish this walk on my feet. I would not get lost. The last thing I wanted was an air rescue instigated by I Told You So Graeme when I was so close to finishing on my own.

The path was getting narrower as I climbed a hill. This didn't seem right. There were gorse bushes all around me until, two hours later, there was no path at all, just a giant clump of bushes that could not be penetrated on foot. Damn those cows. They had tricked me into following a path to nowhere. I was lost. Above me was a black cloud. The wind was howling now. It sounded evil. Did they have hurricanes in Cornwall? I lifted my cell phone to check. No signal.

Circling back, I found another hint of a path, but it just took me to the top of the hill where there were some boulders with a view of more gorse bushes. Sitting down to contemplate my situation, I realised I had no idea where I was or how to get to St Ives. The wind was whipping my hair around and it felt like a cold slap in the face, knocking my dreams of Nara to the back of my mind. THIS was reality. I was a man without a future. I could die right here, and no one would know or care. I was alone, lost and it was a cold cold world. A flash of light and there was an ear-splitting crash as thunder shook the ground. The rain started in fat drops, splashing on the ground.

I waited for another clap of thunder, properly scared, while I considered the idea of praying. My inner cynic whispered in my ear. If you were God, would you answer your prayers? You claimed your religion was science.

'Point taken,' I said. 'But I could be wrong. There have been drastic conversions before. Like Paul. When an angel appeared, he changed his mind.'

And in that very moment, someone did appear, jumping up from the other side of the boulders. My first thought was that it was an angel. He was quite good looking. A trim beard with a hint of grey. Picture Russell Crowe in Gladiator. Then I noted his outfit. Running shorts and a sweatshirt. He was human, just out for a run and untroubled by the weather. Stopping a few feet away from me, his face slick with both rain and sweat, he was breathing heavily. He nodded to me in greeting, a perfect specimen of health and virility.

'Which way is St Ives?' I blurted out.

He threw out his right arm and pointed.

'That way!' And then he carried on with his run, heading the way I had come.

Chapter Eleven

I continued the path to St Ives and in less than half an hour was walking in wet clothes to the centre of town. Another twenty minutes and I finally arrived at the address on my map. A woman was up on a ladder in front of the house, boarding up windows. She was wearing, appropriately enough, a wet suit. Her hair was dripping. There was a surfboard leaning against the house. It was starting to rain harder. Water was cascading down the street. She turned around and stared at me.

'Mr Decker! You made it!'

'Yes! Hello!'

She climbed down the ladder. The rain was suddenly pounding the roof like someone was pouring nails on it. She motioned for me to follow her, and we ran for the front door. I stepped inside and she shut the door behind me and threw the bolt.

'Just in time.'

'Yeah! I guess it's a big one, eh?'

She stared at me like I was daft.

'They're saying this is going to be the biggest storm in a decade. We may be here a while. The power is already out, but don't worry. I have candles. I'm Katie by the way.'

She stuck out her hand and I shook it.

'Nice to meet you, Katie. How long do you think it will last?'

She shrugged and went to the open plan kitchen where she lit the gas stove and put the kettle on. Katie was a short woman, slender but strong-looking, around five feet tall with short blonde hair. She picked up a tea towel and dried it.

'How do you take your tea?' She stopped. 'Ah. You're American. Would you prefer coffee?'

'Yes, I would. Do you have some?'

'Sure. I like coffee too.' As if to explain this she said, 'I spent some time in New York last year.'

'Oh! What'd you think?'

'It was fun. Stimulating. They drink lots of coffee.' She smiled. 'Where are you from?'

'Northern California. Sacramento.'

She made some drip coffee while ruminating on this.

'I take it Northern California is quite different from Southern California.'

'Another country. Like Cornwall is to England.'

She laughed at that. It was a warm laugh. An understanding laugh.

Then there were strange noises, like someone throwing gravel at the windows.

'It's getting bad now, isn't it?' I said.

She stepped to the table where there was a big lantern and lit it. Then she poured coffee.

'We'll be fine.'

And just like that, I knew we would be. Katie was very reassuring.

'Are you a surfer?' I sat down at the table, and she placed the coffee mug in front of me along with a piece of carrot cake she produced from a cupboard. I was sort of relieved that it wasn't chocolate.

'I'm a lawyer most of the time, but I also surf.' She grinned like a little kid. Like she was getting away with something, and I suppose she was. 'The waves were great this morning, but it started getting too rough. Tempting as it was to surf big waves, we have enough rocks here to make it too dangerous in a storm. Do you surf?'

'Me? No. And I've never met a surfing lawyer.'

She sat down across from me with a cup of tea. No cake.

'So, you're a teacher?'

'Not anymore.'

Something about Katie made me feel like talking. We had the whole night ahead of us, so I told her the rambling tale of my being fired. She listened and nodded in all the right places, gave me a refill, and when I was done, she spoke up.

'You know your boss should have given you severance pay. They can't just fire you like that without warning. Documented warning. Especially not now, when you can't even apply to another school for next year.'

She was right.

'What should I do about it?'

Katie shrugged, sipped her tea, and then gave me an appraising look.

'Are you in a union? Or part of a legal association for teachers?'

'No.' I grimaced. 'I probably should have been.'

'A call from your lawyer would clear things up in a hurry.'

I laughed.

'I don't have a–,'

'I'm pretty sure I could get you some compensation pretty quickly, given you're in a foreign country and in need of money.'

'How did you know?'

She shrugged and smiled.

'What do you charge?' I asked.

'This will take about ten minutes. So, let's see,' her eyes were raised to the ceiling. 'That's going to cost you ten quid. Plus, the long-distance charges of five quid.'

Chapter Twelve

I stared at my watch. It was just after nine in the morning in California.

'Is your landline working?'

She pushed back her chair and went to the black telephone on the wall. Lifting the receiver, she gave me a thumbs up. I pulled out my address book from my backpack and there was the number. She dialled and asked for Bill. Her voice turned all legal and bossy. I was scared just listening to her. I could hear the rhythm of Bill's voice explaining the situation, but she was having none of it. She pushed on with her demands. There were numbers. Back and forth. Then an agreement. The sum would go into my bank account. If the money wasn't there by end of the day, she said she would proceed with a legal complaint to the California Court on Monday. She gave him her business number and said he could leave a message for her there when the transfer was complete. Then she hung up. I looked at my watch again.

'That's the most brilliant piece of legal work I've ever seen.'

Katie smiled.

'I got you a year's salary.'

'What?'

'$35,000.'

'How did you know I made that?'

'He told me. He wanted to give you half that, but I told him we'd go for more if he was going to go that way. He knew he was in the wrong. This was an easy fix, and he wasn't stupid.'

'You're good.'

'You'll get my bill for fifteen quid when your ship comes in.'

'Thanks, Katie. I'm speechless. This is the best luck I've had in a long while. Now, could you sort out my love life?'

She laughed again.

'I can give it a try...'

The lights flickered and then went out. We both giggled in the light of the lantern.

'So appropriate. It's more of a ghost story anyway.'

'Go on.'

I told her all about Nara and my dilemma. She smiled and shook her head. 'You aren't the first one to fall in love with her.'

'You know Nara?'

'Everyone knows Nara. You mustn't give up. If she wanted nothing to do with you, she'd leave no room for doubt. She was probably more interested in you than you think. But she was being cautious. You're a tourist after all. An unemployed tourist.'

Katie then stood up and surveyed her kitchen, took out onions, peppers, and mushrooms and put me to work chopping while she opened cans of chopped tomatoes, a jar of tomato sauce and boiled some water. In no time we had a salad and spaghetti and there was some lovely fresh bread to go with it. As we tucked in, she asked me about my plans.

'You know, you should stay a while. You could do that now. Spend some more time with Nara.'

She was right. Now I could do that. I would have some money.'

'How long could I stay on a visitor's visa?'

'Six months. That should be enough time.'

'For what?'

'For you to sort out your love life.' She wiggled her eyebrows.

'You're a romantic.'

'A romantic, surfing, lawyer. Guilty on all counts.'

I shook my head, but hope was coming back to me. Flowing in my veins.

'I'm a photographer,' I confessed.

'Really?'

'Really. Want to see some pictures?'

Before she could answer I had pulled my camera out of my bag and was pushing buttons, showing her what I had taken, including the pictures I took of Nara. She was quiet as she looked, nodding, taking in every detail. We looked at pictures for twenty minutes and she sat back in her chair and stared at me.

'These are... good, Grant. I mean, really good.'

'You're not just saying that because you're my lawyer, are you?'

She snorted and took a drink of her wine.

'In the morning, I'm going to call a friend.'

'A friend?'

'Leslie Stringer. She's on the town council in St Ives. In charge of tourism. She's been looking for a photographer for a while and I think she'll like your work too. She might have some work for you.'

'Damn, Katie. You are really sorting me out!'

She grinned.

'I like sorting people out. It's what I do.'

FIVE YEARS LATER.....

'Daddy, tell me the story.'

'Again?'

'Yeah. Again.'

'But I told you that one last night. Don't you want to hear Goodnight Moon?'

'No, I want the story of you and mum getting married on the beach. When you were Aquaman, and she was a mermaid.'

I gave a little sigh, but in truth, I never tired of telling it.

'OK. Move over.'

I sat down on my daughter's bed, the one I made for her with a half shell headboard. We seem to have a nautical theme running through this family. Katie and I thought it would be a fun idea to get married on the beach in front of St.

Ives, with all our friends and family coming to join us dressed as sea creatures.

Nara was a stunning mermaid, but she couldn't hold a candle to my lovely bride, whom I carried from the car to the spot where we took our vows. Hard to walk in a mermaid's tail. Graeme made an excellent octopus. James came as a walrus. Made his tusks. The boys I'm in the band with at The Kettle and Wink came as sharks. Leslie Stringer who hired me as a photographer came as a hammerhead shark. The Barefoot Nigel and his family just draped seaweed over themselves and were adorable. Nigel was quite at home, barefoot, in the sand.

Even *my* family came from California. And it was a shock, let me tell you, to see my father in a lobster suit and my mother dressed as a squid. My sisters came as a trio of sea horses.

'So, we got married on the shores of St. Ives.'

'I know that, Daddy. But how did you turn into humans? I want to hear that again.'

I knew where this was going. Ariel wanted to believe with all her little heart that she was a mermaid, one that had, for reasons she could not quite fathom, lost her tail and her ability to breathe under the sea.

'Well, it was a rule, that if we wanted to live in this house together and have a child, you, we had to give up our sea life and become humans.'

She trembled.

'Wasn't that hard for you, Daddy? You had to give up your superpowers!'

'Well. Not all my superpowers, pumpkin.'

She laughed, which made my heart sing.

'You can still fly, right?'

I leaned down to speak in her ear.

'Top secret., little mermaid. You can't tell anybody.'

She pretended to button her lips.

I tickled her.

She shrieked. Then turned all serious again, pulling my face in front of her.

'What about me? Do I have any superpowers?'

'You mean, besides being the most amazing person in the whole world and having a mermaid mother and Aquaman dad?'

She smiled at me again, eyes brimming with love.

'Yeah.'

'Well. Let's see. You tell good stories. You draw well. You can almost do a cartwheel. I've seen it.'

'Tracy says it isn't true.'

'What? She hasn't seen your cartwheel then.'

'No! She says it isn't true that you were Aquaman, and mum was a mermaid.'

'Is this the same Tracy who claims to be Santa Claus?'

'Yeah.'

I wrinkled my nose.

'She might not be a reliable source.'

'She doesn't look at all like Santa Claus.'

'I agree. And how does she explain this?'

'Magic. She says she transforms into Santa in December.'

'Uh-huh.'

'You don't believe her?'

'Do you?'

'No. Not really.'

'How come?'

'There isn't a picture of her as Santa Claus.'

'Oh, right.'

'But I have a picture of you and mum. On the beach?'

'Yeah, you do.'

She smiled and yawned.

I put my hand over her eyelids and kissed her cheek.

'Good night, pumpkin. Sweet dreams.'

After closing the door, I came into the front room and plopped down on the sofa beside Katie, who reached for the remote.

'Did she ask to have the story of the wedding again?'

'Yep.'

Katie rolled her eyes and shook her head.

'She's going to be in therapy for years because of that picture.'

'She might just sue us later.'

'Damn. She might. She has a good case. Why didn't you just tell her we were in costumes?'

'I did. Two years ago. But she doesn't want that story. She wants to believe she is special.'

'She IS special. She doesn't need a superhero backstory.'

'Doesn't she?'

Katie sighed.

"What am I going to do with the two of you?'

I pulled her down to the floor, my arms wrapped around her like a giant squid.

'Anything you like, my darling mermaid. Anything you like.'

Acknowledgements:

This is a work of fiction, based on a real walking trip I took on this same coastal route in 2004. That walk had a lasting impact and started me on the path of my writing life. Many thanks to Cornwall and all its characters for inspiring me on this journey.

Thanks to Stephen van Dulken, my husband, for his faith, love, support, and proofreading. Thanks to family and dear friends for their encouragement and to early readers of this story: Deirdre Gainor and Kathie Nielsen. I appreciated the encouragement of the St Leonards-on-Sea Writer's Group, of James Young and the members of that lovely class at the Hastings Bookshop. Thanks to Charlie Crabb, Erica Smith and the creative community in Hastings and St Leonards for the continuous flow of inspiration and connection.

I'm grateful to Dana Brass and Jane Wildgoose for their help. And thank you Tanja Slijepčević for your patient assistance. And thanks always to Lise Patt.

Axel Forrester
Please visit: www.axelforrester.com to learn more about my books, collections, films and collaborations.